CW00857266

First electronic and print editions

Book design by Matthew Goodall

ISBN:
978-0-473-51800-4 (e-pub)
978-0-473-51801-1 (hardback)

Published by Matthew Goodall
www.matthewgoodall.org

To
Stacey.

You
always
have
a
unique
perspective.

Hickory dickory dock

The mouse ran up the clock

The clock struck one

The mouse ran down

Hickory dickory dock.

Hickory dickory dock
The mice ran up the clock
The clock struck two
They checked out the view
Hickory dickory dock.

Hickory dickory dock
The mice ran up the clock
The clock struck three
They watched a movie
Hickory dickory dock.

Hickory dickory dock
The mice ran up the clock
The clock struck four
They ran to the store
Hickory dickory dock.

Hickory dickory dock
The mice ran up the clock
The clock struck five
They started to jive
Hickory dickory dock.

Hickory dickory dock
The mice ran up the clock
The clock struck six
The mice frolic
Hickory dickory dock.

Hickory dickory dock
The mice ran up the clock
The clock struck seven
They turn on the oven
Hickory dickory dock.

Hickory dickory dock
The mice ran up the clock
The clock struck eight
Their dinner was late
Hickory dickory dock.

Hickory dickory dock
The mice ran up the clock
The clock struck nine
They watch the moon shine
Hickory dickory dock.

Hickory dickory dock
The mice ran up the clock
The clock struck ten
The mice are dreaming
Hickory dickory dock.

Hickory dickory dock
The mice ran up the clock
The clock struck eleven
They have a jam session
Hickory dickory dock.

Hickory dickory dock
The mice ran up the clock
The clock struck twelve
They hear the bells
Hickory dickory dock.

Every page has 4 things that rhyme with the number on the clock.

Remember that rhymes don't always sound exactly the same.

Can you find all of them?

Suggested activities:

The pictures have ideas that can be expanded on and explored -

3 monkeys (See no evil, Hear no evil, Speak no evil).
The month of August (8th month), is on the page for '8.'
The seashells can be linked to the tongue twister 'She sells sea-shells by the sea shore.'

There are many other ways to extend this story.
Please share them with us on Facebook: **Matthew Goodall Author**

'Hidden' items

1: bun, sun, London, bacon

2: gnu, poo, menu, canoe

3: zombie, tv, monkey, city

4: door, roar, drawer, snore

5: hive, fries, ties, prize

6: bricks, sticks, tricks (magic), ships

7: melon, penguin, Stetson (hat), button

8: gate, crate, grape, date

9: washing line, pine (tree), sign, twine (ball of string)

10: hen, pen, cayenne, gem

11: dragon, curtain, watermelon, '11' (on cap) / 'XI' (on drums)

12: elf, shelf, smells (from the oven), shells

Lightning Source UK Ltd.
Milton Keynes UK
UKRC010957030520
362630UK00001B/1

9 780473 518011